TEAM TAEKWONDO #3

HOW TO BE CHEERI

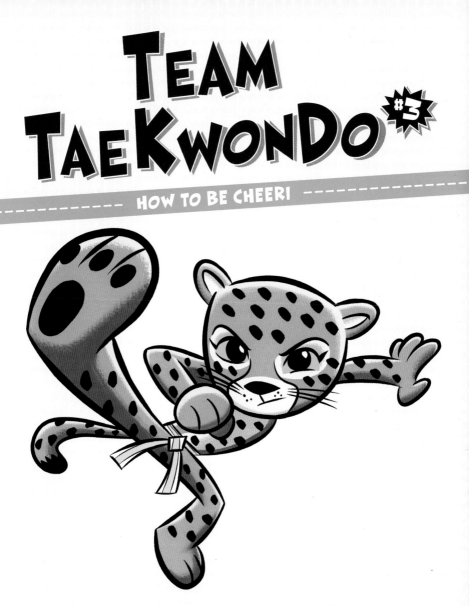

Master Taekwon Lee & Jeffrey Nodelman

Illustrated by Ethen Beavers

RODALE KiDS

RODALE KiDS

This is a work of fiction. Names, characters, places, and incidents either are the product of the author's imagination or are used fictitiously. Any resemblance to actual persons, living or dead, events, or locales is entirely coincidental.

Copyright © 2019 by ATA International.

All rights reserved. Published in the United States by Rodale Kids, an imprint of Random House Children's Books, a division of Penguin Random House LLC, New York.

Rodale and colophon are registered trademarks and Rodale Kids is a trademark of Penguin Random House LLC.

Visit us on the Web! rhcbooks.com

Educators and librarians, for a variety of teaching tools, visit us at RHTeachersLibrarians.com

Library of Congress Cataloging-in-Publication Data is available upon request.

ISBN 978-1-62336-950-7 (hardcover)
ISBN 978-1-62336-948-4 (trade)
ISBN 978-1-62336-949-1 (ebook)

MANUFACTURED IN CHINA

10 9 8 7 6 5 4 3 2 1

First Edition
Random House Children's Books supports the First Amendment and celebrates the right to read.

3

4

5

12

29

44

CLICK!

53

66

68

70

CHAPTER 6

80

I PROMISE:

TO BE A GOOD PERSON,
WITH KNOWLEDGE IN MY MIND,
HONESTY IN MY HEART,
STRENGTH IN MY BODY,
TO MAKE GOOD FRIENDS,
AND...
I WILL BECOME
A BLACK BELT LEADER!

ARA (A-RA)

Ara is a shy turtle. Before joining Team Taekwondo, he usually just stayed in his shell. Now he is making new friends and loves to do his forms nice and slow.

Name means: "of the sea"

Belt rank: white

Favorite move: knife hand strike

BAEOH (BAY-OH)

Baeoh is the funniest tiger ever. He has a big heart and loves to laugh. He is everyone's friend but sometimes lacks confidence.

Name means: "flying tiger"

Belt rank: orange

Favorite move: side kick

CHEERI (CHEER-Y)

Cheeri is the hardest worker in the class. Even though she always makes straight A's, she is always trying hard to get better, maybe sometimes too hard.

Name means: "to defend"

Belt rank: yellow

Favorite move: round kick

RAON (RAY-ON)

Raon is the biggest member of Team Taekwondo. He is very strong and a great athlete. Although he always means well, sometimes he leaps before he looks.

Name means: "lion"

Belt rank: camo

Favorite move: reverse punch

SURI (SUR-Y)

Suri comes from a big family of big eagles. He is small for his age and sometimes tries to act bigger than he really is. He always goes too fast but is working on slowing down.

Name means: "eagle"

Belt rank: green

Favorite move: jump front kick

IOA (CHO-AH)

is a rare phoenix. She is very pretty and likes it when ther animals do things for her. She is learning to do s for herself, and when she does, she is awesome.

e means: "light of the world"

rank: purple

rite move: double knife hand block

MIR (MEER)

Mir is a super smart dragon. He might not be the most coordinated, but he tries really hard. He is learning to control his strength.

Name means: "dragon"

Belt rank: blue

Favorite move: hook kick

RSHA (NAR-SHA)

...a is the nicest cobra you'd ever want to meet.
...hough she doesn't have any arms or legs, she
... of the best in her Taekwondo class. She always
...s hard but keeps a smile on her face.

...e means: "flying high"

...rank: brown

...rite move: tail strike

BARON (BAR-ROON)

Baron is the highest rank in his Taekwondo class. He is a great leader; he just doesn't know it yet. He is always willing to help.

Name means: "righteous"

Belt rank: red

Favorite move: palm strike

MASTER TAEKWON LEE is a seventh-degree black belt and master instructor with many years of experience with ATA International—the world's largest martial arts licensing company. He's also the creator of the award-winning interactive children's video series Agent G. He lives in Little Rock, Arkansas.

JEFFREY NODELMAN is a graphic artist, novelist, painter, and award-winning animator who has worked with Walt Disney, Warner Bros., and Nickelodeon. He is a fourth-degree black belt trained in ATA Songahm Taekwondo and a USA-certified ice hockey coach. He lives in Little Rock, Arkansas, with one wife, two children, and three spoiled rescue dogs.

ETHEN BEAVERS is the illustrator of comics for DC Comics, Dark Horse Comics, and IDW Publishing, as well as numerous kids' titles, including the *New York Times* bestselling series NERDS. He lives in central California. Visit ethenbeavers.com.

THANK YOU FOR READING TEAM TAEKWONDO.

WE HOPE YOU ENJOYED IT!

If you would like to redeem **One Free Class** at a participating independently owned and operated ATA-licensed location near you, please visit:
WWW.ATATIGERS.COM/FREECLASS

One Free Class offer may vary.